# REWIND

# REWIND

## DERIYUN MCGEE

What if there was a cure to cancer and natural diseases?
What if you had a second chance to make the most
important decision of your lifetime . . . What if?

**To order additional copies of this book, contact:**
Xlibris
844-714-8691
www.Xlibris.com
Orders@Xlibris.com
818848

This book is dedicated to my brother Mauriece McGee. The marathon continues. SIP

# CONTENTS

# Chapter 1

## PRESS PLAY

Sitting in the living room, Andre's stressed left hand is slowly massaging his right shoulder with a sort of subdued/zoned-out nervousness. He is watching a news interview on the TV—the reporter is interviewing an individual representing a nonprofit cancer screening group. The interviewee is discussing how the group helps low-income families afford cancer screenings and assistance in treatment costs for chemotherapy. Andre continues to sit on the couch as he stops rubbing his shoulder. He can't quite bring himself to look up at the television; he just stares at nothing toward the bottom corner of the room. He holds his blank stare until the reporter, Stacy, asks how people can help the nonprofit group. The interviewee responds with "Well, we always welcome volunteers to sign up for events or help at our offices, or you can donate." Andre now glances up at the TV. The interviewee continues, "Online or by calling us at 1877 501 0001." An overlay graphic with the number fades onto the bottom of the TV screen.

Andre lifts his phone to his ear. A faint voice picks up, identifying the company. "Yes, hello, I'd like to make a donation. Uh, my name is Andre . . . Jones."

"What was that about, baby?" asks Londa.

"Huh? Oh shit, nothin', just saw something about this organization on the news." Andre responds. Andre stands around five feet nine and weighs around 185 solid with a muscular build. "That big ol' heart of yours strikes again, huh?" Londa replies.

"What you talm 'bout Willis?" Andre asks jokingly. They both laugh then there is a quiet, a peaceful pause.

"You've been extra sweet lately," Londa adds, facetiously skeptical. "You feeling OK?"

"Of course, baby," Andre answers soothingly. There is another brief pause.

Then a subtle solemnness sweeps over Andre. "What would you do . . . ?" he asks Londa.

"What would I do if what?" Londa responds.

"If the doctors gave you that news." He nods at the TV. "What if you only had six months?" Andre asks again, very interested in her answer.

"Well, I would probably wanna get my soul right with God first and foremost. Remember him, Mr. I-Don't-Feel-Like-Going-to-Church-Anymore?" Londa says sarcastically.

"It's only been like a month," says Andre.

"What kind of excuse is that? You've been going every Sunday for how many years?" Londa says in a scornful manner.

"Baby," Andre responds, but Londa cuts him off in midsentence.

"I mean, you do you, but I don't know why—"

Andre interrupts. "I just don't trust these preachers anymore. They be wearing Gucci and driving big cars with rims and stuff. Sometimes I be wondering if God remembers me."

Londa replies calmly, "Dre, you give from your heart without worrying where the money is going, and God will never forget you no matter what you are going through."

Andre is avoiding eye contact and trying to bring his temper down. He knows she's right, but he doesn't want to admit it. Londa looks him in the face and asks, "Is something up with you that I don't know about?"

Andre replies, "No, no. I'm sorry, babe. Everything is OK. I think it's just some of those feelings from losing my pop. I'll be OK. We'll be OK." There's another peaceful pause as they smile at each other.

"I'd fly to Ethiopia," Londa says out of nowhere.

Andre is totally confused. "You'd what?!" he asks loudly.

"If I got sick, I'd fly to Ethiopia where the Ark of the Covenant is," Londa says with a glimmer in her eyes.

Andre jokingly replies, "Oh damn, you like Indiana Jones too? That's my shit!"

Londa shakes her head as she says, "Boy, you ain't been outta church that long!" Londa gets up from the couch and tells Andre, "C'mon, let's go. Dinner on me tonight, in honor of your newfound passion for philanthropy." Londa bents down to kiss Andre.

# Chapter 2

## THE MEETUP

Andre's brother, Deshawn, is at the library, book-signing for his new book. There is a crowd of about five hundred, and the event just started. Deshawn stands about six feet and weighs around 192 pounds. He is very debonair and smooth with a rough edge, being that he, Andre, and his cousin Zack were born in Newtown, Sarasota, Florida. They were born in the old projects off Orange Avenue. "I'm pleased to present to you my new book, *How to Deal with Death and Missing Your Loved Ones*! I'll be honest, this one touched home. I figured I'd share the things that helped me stay strong and keep my head up while dealing with the loss of my loved ones. I'm very thankful for your support. And the books go for fifteen dollars apiece. Thank you." Deshawn wastes no time greeting his customers, shaking hands, signing autographs, and taking money!

Zack walks up with his girlfriend, Maria. Zack is about six feet one and stocky. He weighs around 245 pounds. Maria is five feet five, about 165 pound. She is Latina and definitely older by the looks of it. He wears bright colors most of the time with colored shirts. Zack has a good sense of humor, and he is a very intelligent man. He spends his free time learning about spirituality and healing herbs.

Zack walks to Deshawn's table and interferes. "Excuse me, Mr. Hustler—I mean, Mr. Author." Zack starts laughing. "Oh! What's good, cousin?"

Maria, correcting Zack's rudeness, says, "What he means is he'll take one of everything."

Zack, dismissing Maria, drops the foolishness. "You know I had to come show my cousin some love. Deshawn, you remember Maria?"

"Cuz, y'all been together like six months, not six hours. Yes, I remember Maria." Deshawn redirects his attention to Maria. "Pleasure to see you again. My apologies for having to deal with my cousin."

Maria reciprocates, "Likewise."

Zack asks Deshawn, "How are the book sales?"

Deshawn smirking, discreetly reveals a massive wad of money. Zack jokingly asks under his breath, "Lemme hold something!"

Maria acts like a mom. "Tuh."

Zack corrects himself and replies, "I mean, uh. Great job. Anyway, when you shutting down?"

Deshawn answers, "Like fifteen minutes, cuz."

Zack becomes excited. "Cool, 'cause we're about to grab some grub. Might as well come on—we know you ain't got nobody. Hahaha."

Deshawn gives a disappointed frown that makes Zack laugh harder. Then a voice comes out of nowhere. "Deshawn?"

Deshawn replies "Yes?" before turning and is stunned at who he is seeing.

"Hello, Deshawn. Nice to finally see you face to face," says Desarae. Desarae is a nice-looking, natural sistah.

Deshawn looks mesmerized and confused. "I'm sorry, have we met?"

Desarae looking surprised, "We certainly did. Remember when you slid in my DMs? Or are you just hoppin' in everybody's inbox?" she asked.

Deshawn grins. "I definitely don't hop in everybody's box."

Desarae, subtly seductive, says to Deshawn, "I think it's time we get to know each other—properly."

Zack, being nosy, blurts out, "Girl, you got timing. Me and my chic was coasting while D hit the three-wheel motion." Zack then hits a dance move.

Deshawn ignored Zack and answered Desarae. "I was about to go get some dinner with this fool and his much-too-good-for-him lady."

Desarae asks eagerly, "Would it be too much to ask if I may join?"

Deshawn activates pimp mode. "Who can say no to a dream manifested into a physical form?"

Desarae replies while blushing, "Aren't you quite the wordsmith?"

Zack leans in the conversation and coughs, "Sofathanamufucca." He coughs again as Maria punches him in the stomach playfully.

"Thank you, Maria!" says Deshawn laughingly.

Andre bear-hugs Zack from the side playfully. "You giving my bro shit in front of a pretty lady, cuz?"

Andre releases his grip and pats Zack on his back. "What's good, DJ? Or shall I say, Author Jones!"

Deshawn daps up his brother, Andre. "I'm glad you made it, bruh, and hello, sis. I'm happy to see ya'll still making it," says Deshawn.

"I love my, baby. I ain't going nowhere." She hugs Andre tight, and he grimaces. Andre is clearly in discomfort as Deshawn walks behind him to hug Londa.

Deshawn returns to Andre's side for an introduction. "Everybody, this is Desarae." Desarae smiles and waves as everyone says hello. "Desarae, this is my brother, Andre, and his lady, Londa, and my cousin, Zack, and his lady, Maria."

"Pleasure to meet all of you," Desarae replies.

Deshawn relaxes and is ready to go after a long day. "A'ite, fam. Let me get packed up and let's grab a bite, some drinks, and celebrate. Zack said he's paying."

Zack frowns. "Uh, I got my food. The rest of y'all . . ." Everyone laughs.

"Oh, trust me, I got him." Desarae gestures to Deshawn. "Food and drinks."

Andre is impressed. "Oh, she a keeper, bro," he expresses to Deshawn. Zack is checking out Desarae way too hard. "I agree." Maria smacks him in the back of the head softly.

# Chapter 3

## THE PROBLEM

Interior Restaurant—Evening

Everyone meets up at the restaurant and are seated. Deshawn quiets everyone down at the dinner table. "OK, I gotta joke for everyone. Why did the man take toilet tissue to the Twilight Zone?"

Everyone is trying to figure it out but they give while saying they didn't know at different times.

"Why would he do that," Maria asks.

"Do do do do, do do do do, do dooooo," Deshawn replies with a smirk, mimicking the Twilight Zone theme.

Everyone gives Deshawn a blank stare at first, trying not to laugh. Andre breaks the silence, "Bruh, let Zack be the ignant one." He shakes his head, laughing.

The waitress walks up. "Hey, guys, welcome. Can I start you off with something to drink?"

Zack responds, "Yes, please, we'll take"—he does a quick count—"six bottled waters and six Long Islands." Bartender points at the barback while saying, "Aaaaaaand you owe me ten dollars." The barback makes a bet with the bartender that they would order Hennessey and coke or Heinekens.

Andre says, "Man, why y'all president gotta shut the whole damn government down right when I got hired on my new job? I've been waiting on a damn federal background check two months to start work. That shit finally went through though, and now I start work in two days."

A celebratory burst hits the group.

Deshawn goes in. "Congratulations, bruh!! And I feel you with that 'y'all president' stuff. Don't get me wrong, the man is a G, I ain't gon' lie."

Zack interrupts. "I hope that G stands for giant bully." A murmur of agreement washes over the table.

Deshawn continues, "However, when he said make America great again, that kinda bothered me. The word *again* needs to be examined. What era? Was America great when they enslaved black people? Was America great when they killed up the Indians? When they made segregation legal? When they was hanging blacks from trees and burning 'em alive? When Zimmerman went free after killing Trayvon Martin? Again?"

Desarae adds in. "I can definitely sympathize. But he did get a lot of votes, and he didn't get them for no reason. This president represents the true meaning of being a boss. Do what the fuck he feels, say what the fuck he feels, and tweet what the fuck he feels." Everyone laughs.

Andre chimed in. "I've heard of apples to oranges, but I never heard of oranges to—twitteeer fingers!" Everyone laughs as the waitress comes and serves drinks. Andre and Zack find Desarae's remarks a little odd, perhaps even suspicious, but neither decides to say anything, and both let their qualms go. The waitress walks off.

"You wanna know what's really killing me though? Why we really oughta be mad at the government? We out here dying from diseases that are curable through a change in diet and drinking water with a higher pH balance. Not to mention, there are leads for the cure right in front of our faces. I found out about this plant, moringa, that can cure almost everything. Shit like cancer, aids, heart disease, and all kinds of shit. And you can bet they don't want us having anything to do with that," Zack says.

Andre is visibly irritated. "Man, here you go with this bullshit again. We got the best doctors in the world and the best technology. Y'all gotta let that conspiracy theory shit go."

Londa gave her input. "C'mon, Dre. What you got against alternatives? And since when do you trust anyone with power?" She asked.

Deshawn agreed with Zack. "I mean, Zack does have a point." He said.

Andre looks at Zack. "So now you're turning him on to this bullshit too?"

Zack is exhausted by the thought of more debate. (Andre is heard coughing.)

Zack tried to convince Andre. "Cuz, you haven't even read the shit."

Deshawn tries to soothe things. "Dre, imagine if there was even the slightest possibility that our pops could still be here." Andre is stunned to silence and clearly upset that this subject has come up. Deshawn continues, "Wouldn't you wanna try everything you could?"

Andre is overwhelmed but is trying his best to hold back his emotions. "Excuse me, y'all." Andre rises, grimaces a little, but tries to hide it. Andre walks to the restroom.

Zack looks to Deshawn. "Damn, dog. The fuck is up with Andre, man?" He asked.

Deshawn looks at Zack. "I don't know, cuz. But don't even mention the book we're working on. Tonight ain't the night." He said.

Londa asks inquisitively, "You mean the How to Deal with Death one?" She asked.

Deshawn shaking his head. "Nah, this one is bigger. And actually, the only three people who know about that book are at this table." He said.

Zack is confused. "Three?" He asked.

Desarae clarifies, "Your cousin reached out to me about some of it. I guess my involvement in the medical community caught his interest when he was fishing around profiles and slidin' in people's DMs."

Zack feels a little betrayed. "Damn, cuz. I thought this one was just you and me." He said to Deshawn.

Deshawn tries to recover. "It is, cuz. But, you know, I just wanted . . . an unbiased opinion on a couple things. It's definitely mostly just you and me." He replied to Zack.

Zack sucks his teeth and says, "Whatever, man."

Londa is looking worriedly toward the bathroom. Londa speaks with concern and directs to Deshawn, "Something just doesn't seem right with Andre. I can't tell if it's just still from losing y'all's dad or what, but the last month or so, he's just been a little out of character."

Deshawn replied. "I know, Londa. It's still hitting me too. I think he's just taking it harder or just showing it more."

Zack butted in the conversation. "Well, damn. How can he take a dump in a restaurant? I be scared my ball sack gon' touch the water." He said.

Maria feeling disgusted, asked Zack, "What's wrong with you?! We're at the damn dinner table!"

Zack responded with a quick rebuttal. "I don't see no dinner." He said.

Deshawn decided to excuse himself. "Well, on that note, I'll be right back." Deshawn moves to get up. Inside the restroom, Andre stands in front of the sink, out of breath. Deshawn walks in the restroom. Deshawn is clearly concerned and, with a very straight face, asks, "Andre, what's going on with you, man?"

Andre replied. "I'm good, bro." He coughs and blood spatters the sink. Zack, covering his mouth with his forearm, exclaims, *"Oh shit!"* Andre spins around from the sink, wiping his mouth, irritated, and embarrassed. "I'm fine! Don't worry about me." He said.

Deshawn was concerned, so he spoke up. "Bruh, don't worry about you? Don't play around with your health and tell me not to worry. I don't feel like burying another family member, man. You need to go to the doctor."

Andre washes his hands. "OK, man. Go eat. Damn." Andre continues looking down, aggressively washing his hands and avoiding eye contact. Andre looks worried in the mirror as Deshawn Jones and Zack walk out and wait for him at the door. He smiles, and they walk to the table. Everyone is eating and finishing off their drinks.

Andre walks up and says, "Time to roll out. I will get with ya'll tomorrow, fellas. Nice meeting you, ladies."

Deshawn gave his brother dap and said. "Good night, bruh, talk to you tomorrow. Good night, sis."

Londa replied. "Good night, fam."

Everyone says bye. Andre and Londa leaves.

Zack decided to leave too. "I'm out, cuz, get wit you tomorrow. Nice meeting you, Desarae."

Maria followed Zack's lead. "Nice meeting, ya'll." She said as she left.

Deshawn said his good buys to them also. "Be eazy, cuz, good night, Maria. I'll get with you tomorrow." He said.

Desarae also said good bye. "Good night, ya'll." She turns toward Deshawn. "Now I got you all to myself."

Deshawn smiled. "So tell me more about yourself. What do you do for a living?" He asked?

Desarae reveals a slight devilish grin, "I'm a caretaker. But I'm going to school to be a RN."

Deshawn complimented her. "A woman with goals. I like it. Appreciate you hangin'. Sorry about my fam . . . we've kinda been going through it." He said.

Desarae replied. "Don't worry, I get it. And that was nothing compared to some of the horrible first dates I've been on." Deshawn is clearly happy to hear this is a date. "You obviously love each other very much. Something I've been missing out on in life for a long time."

Deshawn responded. "How would you like to maybe work on changing that tonight?"

Desarae gave in. "So far, I'd say we're off to a pretty good start. What do you say we make it a good finish and have a nightcap at my place?" She asked. Deshawn's curiosity is clearly piqued. Desarae reaches toward Deshawn. Her hand gently but sensually grabs the second button from the top of Deshawn's shirt. Desarae beckons Deshawn with her finger to follow. Deshawn slowly concedes.

"You know, I'm usually more of a leader, however . . . I like the view from back here." Deshawn said.

Desarae grins. "You ain't seen nothing yet." They exit the restaurant.

## Desarae's Apartment—Night

Desarae enters the apartment first, walking with purpose. Deshawn slowly enters with a sense of mild impairment.

Desarae welcomes Deshawn in. "Home sweet home." She said

Desarae walks over to her in - house bar. "White or spiced?" She offered?

Deshawn makes himself at home, flopping on the couch. "I like the sound of spiced—and thank you." He replied.

Desarae pours a brown liquor over ice in a rocks glass. She walks the drink over to Deshawn. Deshawn is on the couch looking Desarae up and down as she hands him his drink. Deshawn snaps back to attention to receive the beverage. He takes a sip, surprised by how good it is.

Deshawn says to her. "Damn, you got the good stuff!"

Desarae replied quickly. "Oh, baby, I got the best stuff."

Deshawn examines the mysteriously delicious liquor in his glass. "What is this, girl?"

Desarae slowly begins walking away, brushing her hand on Deshawn's shoulder. "I took a bit of a working vacation down to Cuba recently. Might've brought some contraband back with me."

Deshawn is still looking at his drink; he takes another sip or two then says, "I see, you got a lil bad in you."

Desarae seductively peers back at Deshawn, biting her lip. Deshawn stares toward the coffee table with a solemn look. Desarae continues to walk away.

"I'll be right back. Make yourself at home." She says to Deshawn.

Deshawn breaks his zoned-out gaze and is now focused on a book on the coffee table. He notices a curious envelope under the book. Deshawn looks down as he takes a sip of his drink and begins leaning forward, curious to see what is on the envelope.

Desarae's silhouette comes to occupy the doorframe behind Deshawn. She's striking a pose in the doorway, wearing lingerie. Desarae says to Deshawn, "Hey you." Deshawn turns around as he looks at her in semi-drunk amazement. He blinks twice. "Let me help ease your mind for tonight." She said. She turns up the music.

Deshawn happily replied. "Well, damn." He sips drink in awe as Desarae dances provocatively. Desarae grabs him by the tie and leads him to the room and throws Deshawn down onto the bed and begins to climb on top of him. Desarae kisses Deshawn's lips, and she straddles him. "Did you think you were going somewhere?" she asks.

"I'm here, baby. I ain't going nowhere," Deshawn replies. They begin kissing, and Deshawn flips Desarae on her back then takes off his shirt and clothes. Desarae begins taking off her clothes, and Deshawn helps her. Needless to say, Deshawn gave Desarae the real business that night.

# Chapter 4

## THE NEXT DAY

Desarae and Deshawn is asleep in bed. Deshawn's phone starts ringing, and it wakes him up. Deshawn hurriedly grabs and answers the phone. Deshawn, whispering, says, "Hey, sup, bro, how is everything?"

"Why you whispering, bro?" Andre asked.

"Don't worry 'bout that. What did the doc say?" Deshawn replied.

"Man, put some clothes on. You and Zack need to meet me at the Sixth Street Park." Andre demanded.

Deshawn responded. "10-4, bro, gimmie like an hour."

Andre intensely asks again, "Why. Are. You. Whispering?"

Deshawn ignored his question again. "See you in a hour, bro." Deshawn hangs up. Desarae sits up and leans over to embrace Deshawn.

Desarae asks Deshawn. "You leaving me already? I wanted to cook us some breakfast."

Deshawn gets up and begins putting on his clothes. "Don't worry." He then, against all better judgment, does his Terminator impersonation. "I'll be back," he says in his Arnold voice.

Desarae is squeamishly amused. "Lawd have mercy, that was so lame."

Deshawn leaves.


At the Park

Andre is sitting on a table. He looks shell-shocked and numb. Deshawn and Zack approach Andre from behind.

Zack greets Andre. "Aye, what up, cuuuuz!"

Andre appears annoyed by Zack's cheerfulness.

Deshawn got right to the point. "Talk to me, brother. You good?" Andre just drops his head down and looks at the ground. He said.

Zack followed up behind Deshawn. "C'mon, man. Wassup? I'm supposed to be eatin' waffles and shi—"

Andre is still looking down. "I got cancer, man."

Deshawn and Zack are stunned. Simultaneously, Deshawn and Zack both say, "Oh no." Everyone is still and silent.

Deshawn encourages Andre. "We can beat this, bruh. People are getting healed with natural herbs and foods and a diet change."

Andre just lets out a worn "Nah."

Zack, who didn't even hear Andre's response, says, "Yeah, plus that moringa plant cures cancer." Andre, still looking down, is just barely shaking his head while Deshawn and Zack's outpouring of ideas continues.

Deshawn continued trying to convince Andre. "Exactly, bro. Those two together, plus all the stuff we've been researching for the book—"

Andre, who can't take anymore, finally looks at Deshawn and Zack and snaps back, "It's a lot fucking worse than you think, bruh. I got a biopsy coming up, but it's a done deal. We ain't got time for magic plants and experiments and shit, bruh. I need chemo. I can beat this shit, man. But I need y'all's support, not your ideas."

Deshawn responded. "This is the support, bro." He said.

Zack advises Andre. "We at least gotta try the natural remedies, cuz."

Andre snapped back. "Y'all doctors all of a sudden? 'Cause that's what I need—doctors. They know what they doing. I'm putting my life in the hands of professionals, not a bunch of bored motherfuckers with YouTube channels." He said.

Zack replied. "Cuz, I feel you, but you trusting the same motherfuckers that made this shit. Michael Jackson and Tupac told us, they don't give a fuck about us. They're making money by making us sick. They don't want you to focus on natural remedies."

Deshawn chimes in. "Zack is right, bro. Please give it a shot. We've been researching this shit for over a year now."

Andre is no longer angry, just tired. "I don't have time to be experimenting. My life is at stake here. I'm going back to the doctor's office Friday. They gon' perform surgery and maybe see if they can remove it. They say I have throat cancer. If it's already moved throughout my body, then shit is gonna get hella real."

Deshawn still tried to convince Andre to go natural. "Damn, bruh. I'm with you man, but it won't hurt to at least take the holistic approach and see the doctors too."

Andre looks toward the horizon. "Don't worry about me, bro, I'mma beat this shit, I'mma soldier."

Everyone parts ways.

## Deshawn's Home

Deshawn is deeply focused on his reading. A chaotic spread of books, notes and notepads lay before Deshawn on the desk. Deshawn, now home at his dining room table, is still intensely reading and searching the internet. Deshawn's eyes frantically scan the page. Intensity builds as he continues to read. Deshawn throws the book due to feeling infuriated by defeat. "Fuck!" he yells. Deshawn buries his head in his hands. "I can't believe my brother has five months to live." He said out loud.

# Chapter 5

## FIVE MONTHS LATER

In Home Hospice

Andre is in bed, and Londa is seated in a chair beside him. A gentle knocking is heard at the open doorway. Deshawn is standing in the doorway; slowly he makes his way inside. Londa, beside Andre, waves Deshawn in and forces a smile through tears. Londa stands to hug Deshawn. Londa's voice breaks as she whispers, "I don't know how I'mma keep going without him."

Deshawn trying to be strong, replied. "You gon' live, sis."

Deshawn's arrival causes Andre to stir. Andre struggles to sit up. His body is worn, and his reactions and motor functions have been decimated by his disease. Andre, incredibly labored, manages to wheeze out the name "Deshawn . . ."

Deshawn is fighting back tears. "What up, brodi?" He asked.

Andre feebly reaches his arms out for Deshawn. They embrace and a smile slowly crawls across Andre's face. It looks like it takes the same amount of effort for him to smile as it would take anyone else to do a sit-up. Andre begins to speak, mustering all the energy his body doesn't have. His speech is painfully labored, with each syllable causing visible strain to his body. "I should have listened. Thank you for trying to help me." He slowly nods toward Deshawn.

Deshawn replied. "You welcome bruh. Don't worry about that man."

Andre just shakes his head slowly with a small smile, trying to soothe his brother. Andre says, "I'm ready." Andre looks up toward the sky with a faint nod. Deshawn begins to cry but Andre stops him before he can shed a tear. Andre whispers, "Don't cry, bruh." Andre's stare begins to become unfocused and his breaths shorter and more infrequent.

Deshawn begins to pray. "Dear heavenly Father, Yahweh, in the name of Yeshua, may your will be done. Please wrap your protection around his spirit and guide him, for we know you have the last say so. Amen." Andre is clearly slipping from this realm. Deshawn is keeping a strong face, but yet the pain is seeping through his scowl. "I'm wit ya, bruh. I love you, man. 420, 3.6.T forever, bruh."

Andre, with his last earthly breath, can only mouth the words, but it's more than enough—"I love you." Andre goes into a deep sleep. And Deshawn doses off in the chair next to the bed. His breathing goes slower and slower until it stops. Deshawn is woken up by Londa.

Londa struggles to get the words out. "He gone, bruh." She informed

Deshawn has been mentally and spiritually preparing himself for this moment. He remembers everything his grandmother and grandfather taught him about the kingdom of the Most High God, Yahweh. He felt a calmness in his spirit because Andre is now with the Lord, and there is no place better.

Deshawn with tears in his eyes, says his goodbye to his brother. "Tell Mama and Granddad I love em. I'll see you when I get there, bruh."

# Chapter 6

## THE MISSION

Zack and Deshawn meet up at the park the next day. Zack asks, "How you holding up, bro?"

"Just keeping my faith in the Lord. I know God don't make mistakes. Shit just crazy, man. I lost my mom, granddad, dad, and now my bro is gone. Only thing keeping me positive is faith. I know the spirit never dies. Better to be with God than be here with me," Deshawn answers.

"I'm glad you in good spirits, man. 'Cause I think this shit is fucked up, man. I can't believe Dre is gone, cuz. You not gon' believe what I'm 'bout to tell you." Zack informed Deshawn.

"What's that, cuzzo?" Deshawn asked?

Zack started off slowly. "I ran into a former coworker with stage 3 cancer a couple months before Andre died. I got to talking with her about all that shit we've been studying—and she totally bought into it, right? I gave her the plant, I helped set her up on a diet, tried a mix of different medicines. I just talked to her after she left the doctors yesterday, bruh. No cancer. The doctors had her on chemo and shit, now they're fuckin' baffled, and they wanna do all kinds of tests and shit. We fucking did it. I mean, obviously there's more to do, but we are one hundred percent onto something huge, cuz."

Deshawn is absolutely floored. "Zack, the shit really works?!" He asked Zack.

Zack replied. "Shit yeah, bro! We gotta finish that fucking book!"

Deshawn's excitement seems to be more fury than happiness. "You mean to tell me we had the cure the whole time, and my brother is dead?" He asked with anger in his voice.

Zack trying to stay excited, responded to Deshawn. "Well, yeah, D. I mean, your brother made his mind up. It's not our fault we lost him. Cuz, we're onto something that will guarantee no family has to ever go through that fucked-up shit ever again!"

Deshawn is overflowing with rage. "He trusted those fuckin' doctors and this fucked up government, and now he's dead! My brother is fucking dead, Zack!"

Zack still tried to calm Deshawn down. "Bro, I feel you. But, like, what you gon' do about it? What can you do about it? You know whoever owns the pharma companies run this country." He stated.

Deshawn's phone rings, interrupting the conversation. Deshawn answers the phone. "Author Jones speaking . . . Yes, I am . . . Let's do it at my home . . . OK . . . Two p.m. tomorrow? Perfect . . . OK, thank you, Stacy . . . You too . . . Bye." Deshawn hangs up and stares at the phone intensely, suddenly rid of his furious stress. He looks at Zack with intense thought. "You wanna know what I'm gonna do?"

Zack pauses. "Shit, do I?" He asked?

Deshawn looks across the horizon. "They enslaved us in 1619. Over four hundred years, cousin. Over *four hundred years*!"

Deshawn collects himself after the small outburst then continues, "First, our chains were physical then Willie Lynch taught this country how to make a slave. They cut our tongues out so we couldn't speak our language. They killed us if they caught us reading or writing. They did everything to erase our story and replace it with history. You shall know the truth, and the truth shall set you free. You helped me see the truth and now I'm free. It's only right I set our people free. These motherfuckers killed my brother. And tomorrow, I'm gonna bring down their fucking world. I'm gonna kill them with the truth."

Zack looks at Deshawn. "To whom much is given, much is expected. But how are you gonna pull this grand scheme off?" He asked.

Deshawn answered him. "They just gave me a live television audience to bust it open to." Deshawn walks away to his car. Zack just sits there and watches Deshawn walk away.


## Desarae's Apartment—Sunset

Deshawn is walking up to Desarae's building with flowers in hand. Two men in black suits walk toward Deshawn in the hallway. They seem to be beelining it for Deshawn, but once they reach him, they only look at him and continue walking. Deshawn turns his head and watches them as they continue to walk off. Deshawn rings Desarae's doorbell.

Desarae answered the door. "Hey, hunny, come on in!" Desarae begins beaming when she sees the flowers. Deshawn enters and takes off his shoes and blazer.

"How was your day, babe?" Deshawn asked.

Desarae replied. "My day was . . . eventful, I suppose. How are you holding up?"

"I'm here." Says Deshawn.

"Aww, honey, would a massage help you unwind? Perhaps after I feed you?" Desarae asked.

"I would love to, but I have to go home and get ready for tomorrow. I just booked an in-home interview, so I gotta tighten up my place before they get there. I just wanted to pull up on ya and check on you." Deshawn expressed to Desarae.

Desarae responded. "How you gon' just pop in and leave like that? C'mon, I already got dinner ready."

Deshawn gave in easily. "A'ight, I'll take a few bites and a couple sips, baaaby." He said.

Desarae escorts Deshawn into the dining room and they sit down to have dinner.

Desarae congratulates Deshawn. "So congrats on your interview tomorrow! Not surprised, just surprised they didn't call you sooner. You are the only author I know that has sold over 150,000 books. And they're not just selling in America. How does that make you feel being a successful black author that made it out the jungle?"

Deshawn replies, quoting A Boogie wid da Hoodie, "Dat jungle turned me to a monster, that jungle made me go harder."

Desarae sings along, "This is what dat jungle do."

Deshawn explains to Desarae. "I went from selling nicks to dimes to quarters to halves to ounces to pounds to, well . . . you get the picture. If you can make it in the hood, you can make it anywhere."

Desarae likes what she hears. "Toast to that." She says.

Deshawn says with a wave of seriousness, "I gotta tell you something." Desarae looks over at him with attention. "They need to pay for what they did to my brother."

Desarae is clearly confused. "What? Andre died of natural causes, baby. Who has to pay for what happened to him?"

Deshawn replies with confidence, "Channel 8 tomorrow. Live."

Desarae is clearly dismayed. "Deshawn, I think you need to stick to writing books and maybe taking some of your own advice from them. You've been goin' on about some secretive vendetta and plot for revenge against I don't know what. Move forward with me, and we can grow old together one day. And you know what, you've got clothes here. Enough of this crazy talk. You're staying here tonight."

Deshawn, who is pretty much in his own world, didn't hear a word Desarae just said. "Sun Tzu, baby."

# Chapter 7

# LET 'EM KNOW

## Deshawn's Home—Setup for Interview—Late Afternoon

"Good evening and welcome to another edition of *The McGee* show. As always, I am your host, Stacy McGee. Tonight, we have an incredibly special guest. He is a best-selling author who has previously been listed on the *New York Times* best-seller list, and tonight, he will be discussing his newest book *How to Deal with Death and Missing Your Loved Ones*. We are very honored to have him tonight, Author Deshawn Jones. Mr. Jones, thank you so much for joining us tonight."

Deshawn smiles. "Thank you for having me, always a pleasure." He says to Stacy.

"So give us a little background on your new book, *How to Deal with Death*." She says to Deshawn.

Deshawn responds. "I wrote this book in hopes of assisting those who are finding it difficult to deal with loss in their own lives by pulling from the experiences of loss I've had in mine. When I began writing, I was going through a lot of traumatic losses myself. I dedicated this book to my mom, dad, grandfather, and my brother, Andre Jones, whom I lost this year. None of those were easy losses, but I feel that the best way to deal with death is to focus on life."

"Focus on life to deal with death?" Stacy repeats Deshawn.

Deshawn continues. "The more we can appreciate and embrace life, whether current or past, the easier it is to see that there are bigger things in motion. The spirit never dies. To be out of body is to be in the presence of God."

Stacy leaned forward. "Very interesting perspective, Mr. Jones. I do want to say I am sorry for your losses and especially sorry to hear about the recent loss of your brother." She said.

Deshawn replied. "Thank you, Stacy. I lost my brother to cancer. My brother was a great man. He was my hero growing up, and even through his transition, he remained strong, and you know what, Stacy? He didn't have to die."

"What makes you say he didn't have to die? Is that referring to lifestyle choices he could have made to prevent the disease?" Stacy asked.

"We can all make better choices to improve our health or at least reduce our odds of getting cancer. But that's not what I meant in regard to his unnecessary passing. What I'm saying is that my brother found out he had cancer, and he, unfortunately, decided to trust the treatment options pushed by doctors who make their money pushing those 'solutions.' Meanwhile, we had a holistic approach that could have pushed his cancer into total remission. A lot of these doctors only care about money, and most of the rest don't care to know any better. But what are they going to do? I feel like most deadly diseases are made by the government in a lab somewhere. Some rich billionaire with glasses on is behind the scenes somewhere plotting population control tactics.

Stacy, now clearly taken aback, is getting nervous and skeptical. "That is an awfully strong statement."

"I know it is. You want an even bolder one? Moringa plants cure cancer. My brother trusted the lies that he was educated on, and those same lies killed him! Meanwhile, moringa holds the cure to cancer. They call it a dietary supplement. I hope you all do your research. It can be bought at any whole-food store or even grown in your backyard. It holds the cure to over three hundred diseases, including AIDS. And that's all coming in my next book—and you can almost guarantee the *New York Times* won't even be able to ignore this one, no matter how bad they want to." Deshawn boasted.

Stacy frantically tries many times to interject, but she is unsuccessful. "Well, we appreciate your insight on the matter. I'm Stacy McGee. We will be right back after these messages."

Stacy looks stunned and is maybe kinda pissed. "Well, Deshawn, that isn't exactly the interview I expected today."

Deshawn smiled. "Well, I really enjoyed myself and appreciate the platform. We should do another one soon." He said.

Deshawn winks and walks out of the room as Stacy's cell phone rings. Stacy walks out the house, muffled in the phone, saying, "Well, how the fuck was I supposed to know he was going to say that?!"

## Deshawn's Apartment—Next Morning

Deshawn is in his kitchen, phone against ear, waiting for the other end to pick up.

Desarae's mind is obviously elsewhere when she answers, "Hello?"

Deshawn excitedly says, "Hey, baby, I was calling you all night! Have you been trying to get through to me?"

Desarae is annoyed. "No, I haven't."

Deshawn is too high on life to notice her obvious discontent demeanor. "Huh, weird. I keep getting calls, but they keep dropping before anyone says anything. I thought it must've been you. Anyway, you see the news, baby?"

Desarae is now plainly mad. "Yeah, Deshawn, I saw it. You cured cancer? Are you out of your fucking mind?"

Deshawn is still brushing off her mood. "Baby, I told you. I told you I had something big, and I was gonna bust them wide open."

Desarae suddenly became enraged. "You don't have shit, Deshawn! You have no studies, no trials. All you have is some of the most powerful people in the world staring you down. And I begged you not to do this. I begged you." She said. Deshawn was bewildered. "You serious, Dez? He asked. You know there's more to what I got—"

Desarae cuts him off. "I know that I wish I wasn't involved in it. That's what I know, Deshawn. You really shouldn't have done that. Goddammit, I really wish you hadn't done that." Desarae hangs up.

Deshawn was puzzled. "You fucking serious, Dez? Hello? Hello?! Man, fuck!" Deshawn hangs up, and his screen goes to black. Deshawn's phone rings again; his screen returns. He picks up so fast he doesn't even look at the name. "Baby, I'm sorry—"

Zack surprised and disgusted replied, "The fuck? You gay?"

Deshawn begin to speak. "Wha—?" Deshawn checks phone "Shit. Man, shut up."

Zack in all seriousness said. "Meet me at the park. Now."

Deshawn asked "What'chu mean now?"

Zack yelled. "I mean right now, dog! Damn!" Both hang up. Deshawn leaves to meet with Zack.

## Park—Evening

Deshawn is looking at his phone. Zack walks up and says, "Damn, you really went viral."

Deshawn replies, "Yeah, and I'm sure these Big Pharma motherfuckas got an eye on me now."

Zack felt like Deshawn was being selfish. "You, nigga? What about me? Why you think I called you out here? I swear there's a Crown Vic circling my block every thirty minutes." Zack said.

Deshawn looked concerned but then his face transformed. "People need to know the truth"

Zack "What about me, cuz? You see what they do to any black man that steps up to save the people? I didn't ask for this shit. I just wanted to write a book with you."

Deshawn puts his phone down, stops walking, and looks up to avoid the conversation from continuing. He's surprised by what an easy out he's about to get.

Deshawn asked Zack. "Cuz, is that Boscoe over there?"

Boscoe is about six feet two, and he weighs three hundred pounds. He is a very rough-looking character being that he had one big-ass dread on his chin. Boscoe, Zack, and Deshawn grew up in the projects together. Boscoe was a known hitta in his neighborhood growing up and it was rumored that he caught over 20 bodies. He was the man known as the grim reaper at one point and time. At one point, they all hustled together. Boscoe was popped in the operation one drop in Sarasota by the feds back in the day and now he is out.

Deshawn also mentions, "I thought he was still servin' fed time. What the fuck?"

Boscoe is up on the street corner. He sees Deshawn and Zack and starts heading over.

Zack speaking low says.

Zack states, "Only one way to get outta time like that."

Deshawn laughs, "Boi, you smell like Velveeta."

Boscoe walks up and speaks. "Long time no see, fellas." He said.

Deshawn speaks back. "Welcome home." He said.

Boscoe obliged. "'Preciate it."

Zack got straight to the point. "Who you snitched on, nigga? I heard you working wit the feds, nigga. What the fuck you want over here? I ain't trying to be seen round you, nigga. Bad enough I'm with this motherfucker right here." Zack gestures to Deshawn.

Boscoe frowns at Zack. "Can't believe everything you hear, nigga. Deshawn, I need to have a word with you."

Deshawn wasn't trying to be seen around Boscoe. Deshawn replied, "I can't help ya, bruh. But the police academy accepting applications." Zack starts to laugh.

Boscoe frowned at that statement. "Ha-ha, real funny, nigga. But for real, I need to tell you what's going on." Boscoe knew Deshawn was a good guy with a dark side if provoked. Boscoe also knew that Zack will kill anyone for fucking with Deshawn.

Deshawn asked Boscoe, "What you need to tell me, bruh?"

Boscoe is looking around nervously. Boscoe hesitates then says, "It's a blessing to have powerful enemies. Keep doing God's work. But just remember, do God's work long enough and you're bound to come against the devil." Boscoe walks off. Deshawn and Zack both look very concerned.

Zack breaks down laughing. "What the fuck kinda shit was that? Goddamn, prison got him all kinds of fucked up." Zack keeps laughing.

Deshawn is still concerned. "Aite, cuz. I gotta bounce. I'll catch you later."

Zack, still laughing, is now picking at Boscoe. "'Do the work of God, you'll have to battle Satan, ha ha ha." Deshawn and Zack carefully watch Boscoe walk away. Deshawn gave Zack dap and walks away from the park, phone to ear.

Deshawn left a voice message. "Hey, baby, I really could use a call from you. I'm headed to the barbershop, but I'll call you when I'm done, Bye."

# Chapter 8

## CONSEQUENCES

The same two FBI agents Deshawn saw at Desarae's apartment are riding in a black Dodge Charger, and they pull up next to Boscoe.

FBI Agent 2 says to Boscoe, "Get in the car."

With a straight face, Boscoe looks around as if he wants to run, but he gets in the car.

Agent Nueman was driving. He looked straight at the road as he spoke to Boscoe. "I'm not going to pretend to know what you're thinking, because the truth is, I don't really give a fuck. Do you know where you stand on the proverbial food chain?"

Agent Nueman looks like a character taken out of *Men in Black*. He wears a crew cut and stands about five feet nine. He has a muscular build and reminds you of the one bad guy in *The Matrix*. Boscoe looks uneasy with adrenaline-spiked confusion.

Agent Nueman continues speaking. "The truth is, you were the best bad decision available, and subsequently, you made the worst good decision you could because you didn't know any better. And now you're stuck between a rock and a dragon."

Agent Nueman is amused by his witty realization and turns around to Boscoe in the backseat of the car. "Funny, isn't it rocks that landed you in there in the first place?" He asked while looking in the rearview mirror at Boscoe. He pulls off the main road into a wooded area while driving down a dirt road.

Boscoe is unamused, but remains silent.

Agent Nueman, realizing his words are only serving to stroke his ego, continues, "There are wheels in motion that would blow your fucking mind to try and understand—and that's if I didn't blow them out of your head first myself.

The *truth* is, I don't look at the world like you do. I don't see what you see. What do you see, Mr. Woods?"

Boscoe is hesitant, confused, and slightly defensive that the agent used his last name. "What'chu mean 'what I see'?"

Agent Nueman turns to look at Boscoe in the backseat. "When you look at my face. What do you see?"

Boscoe is still confused as hell and uneasy. "I see a Remington Steel looking ass muthafuka, got damn Owen Wilson wit a nose job, Luke Wilson face ass cracka."

Agent Nueman, flippantly responds as he turns back around to face forward: "You see, *that's* what I'm talking about. Everyone sees this world, and they see the people in it, and they see niggers, spics, *crackers*, Christians, Muslims." He pauses and takes a breath. "They don't see what's important." Boscoe officially has no clue what the fuck is going on. Agent 1 continues. "They don't see the *perpetual motion machine* because they can't recognize the chaos in which it thrives, weaving around us, ripping *through* us, and taking as much or as little energy as it pleases"—he flicks his fingers forward into space—"and fucking off however it pleases."

Boscoe's anxiety is turning to irritation. *"What the fuck did you say!?"*

Agent Nueman continued, "The world doesn't give a shit who you are. Doesn't give a shit what color you are, how much money you have, or what you do with the meat-sack you inhabit. But the society I'm working for and the machine that now owns you—they care even less." Agent 1 looked like he came out of an action movie like the Avengers. He was Caucasian and stood about 5'9 weighing about 205 pounds of solid muscle. His hair was black and shiny in a crew cut. He had a smooth face. He wore an all black suite, white shirt, black tie, and black sunglasses.

Agent Holdman is not of many words. He stands six feet three he looks like a mixture of white and Puerto Rican. He slowly turns around. "Why didn't you do it? We let you out of your cage for one little favor, and you ruined it. We interrupt the news—black man found dead in bushes at the park, eaten by alligators—wait, gators don't like dark meat..."

The agents look at each other in disgust. Car comes to a halt. They play a game of rock-paper-scissors. Agent Holman losses. He flicks off Agent Nueman. He turns around and shoots Boscoe twice, one in the chest and one right between the eyes...... "I guess the ops will be smoking Boscoe tonight he said with a sinister grin."

# Chapter 9

## TIME'S UP

### Barbershop

Deshawn walks in the barbershop and takes a seat. The female Hairstylist was an Afro Indian that was BBW in stature with an hourglass figure, her hips were like 2 feet apart. Deshawn couldn't help but to stare her. She had pecan tan complexion with white manicured nails. She whispered to her customer, "Ain't that him?" Hairstylist's customer, smiling at Deshawn replied, "Yes, giiiirl, that is him!" Deshawn pretended not to hear them, but he smiled and waved as he walked by. Deshawn was bowlegged so he had this walk that looked like he was floating in slow motion. The ladies were mesmerized by his appearance, but they kept it together. The barbers were having a discussion when Deshawn walked in. He sat down to listen to the barbershop talk. The only white barber in the barbershop began talking. He was close to 40, he was a chubby guy with a trimmed and razor edged beard. "Man, I'm telling ya'll, times have of changed. Not all of us was raised to be hateful and racist. Shit, I grew up right here in the Old Projects. I got beat up because I was white, but my other black friends stood up for me. I realized the difference between an ideology versus what's really wrong and right. We get pulled, and they let me go free but took my homies to jail. We was together and still I had privilege. Yeah, I'm protesting too because it's time for change man." He said. His customer nods his head in agreement while sitting in the waiting area.

The Owner of the barbershop had a customer also. He replied to the other barber. "You and these conspiracy theories, you gon' mess around and have 'em come looking for you!" The barbershop owner wakes up his customer. "Wake up, man. Go rinse some water on your face. I'm trying to cut your damn hair."

His customer gets up, yawning. He had to be like 17 maybe. He looked like he had been popping pills and he smelled of alcohol. He was thin and stood about

5'9. He was an Afro Indian also. He looked around and said to both the barbers, "All this boring talk put me to sleep in this motherfucker. All ya'll talk about is black this and black that, but ya'll sleep because I know what really matters the most!" He gets up and starts walking to the restroom. His pants are skinny, but they sag. You can also see his boxers hanging over the top of his skinny jeans. The barbershop owner asks him, "What's that, bro?" His customer replied. "Deeeeeez nuuutsss!" He starts laughing profusely as he walks to the restroom. The other barber shakes his head as he motions for Deshawn to come to him. "Come on, I'll cut your hair." He said to Deshawn. Deshawn looks around and says, "Man, I'll wait. You ain't finna fuck my shit up." He replied. "Wooow, really, Mista Author!" He throws his hands up. Deshawn laughs and says, "Aite, aite." Deshawn he sat in the barber's chair. The barbershop owners customer comes out of the restroom and leaves the door open. The barbers yell at him about leaving the door open because it smells. The customer has a brown streak on his paints in the center of his butt. The barbershop owner stops him from sitting down and yells, "Ohh nooooo, you ain't sitting in my chair, lil stanky booty ass boy!!!" He turned his chair away from the customer.

Deshawn begins laughing, but quickly tapers off when his attention is pulled to a smaller mirror on the counter. Deshawn is instantly worried because he sees those same two agents approaching the barbershop. Deshawn's eyes go super wide as he sees the agents looking directly at him. Deshawn jumps out of the chair. They quickly draw and fire two rounds each. The other barber gets hit in the neck with a shot. Deshawn stays low and scrambles out the back of the shop. The two agents turn to look at each other. They start a round of rock-paper-scissors. Agent Nueman starts off. "One, two, three, shoot," Agent Holdman sticks his middle finger in Nueman's face, smiles, and starts in the barbershop after Deshawn.

Agent Nueman, obviously annoyed, begins running up the street. Deshawn is in the alley, panicked and trying to dial his phone. He turns up a passage and hides while he impatiently waits for his call to be answered. Agent Holdman enters the alley with a calm intensity. Deshawn is still panicked when the other end picks up. "Baby! Where are you?" He asked frantically. Desarae replied, I'm, on 11th and MLK. "Oh my God, perfect. I need your help, no time for questions. Pick me up on Thirteenth." Deshawn pockets the phone and bolts from cover. Agent Holdman sees him and quickly draws and fires a shot. Deshawn screams as the shot ricochets off the dumpster by his head. Agent Holdman calmly lowers his weapon and begins a light jog, with almost a little dance in his step.

Desarae pulls up in her car and jumps out, approaching the end of the alley. Deshawn reaches out to her and embraces her as he is exhausted and out of breath. Deshawn, panicking, says, "We got—we gotta go! We gotta go. We—"

Desarae hugs Deshawn and says. "No, you gotta go." The smooth and unmistakable sound of a silenced gunshot is the only sound heard as Deshawn's eyes go wide with shock.

Desarae says with a sad look on her face, "It's OK, baby. Some of us get into the house. Some of us never leave the field. I'm sorry, Deshawn." Deshawn falls from Desarae's arms onto the ground. A pool of blood forms around Deshawn, and Desarae gets into her car and drives off. As Deshawn lays there, he has flashbacks of his family and his brother. He didn't think his life would end this way. In his short gasps for breath, he manages to say, "Lord, forgive me for my sins. Please accept me into your kingdom in the name of Yashua."

His eyes slowly closes, and Deshawn dies alone without anyone around that loved him—a cold lonely death because he wanted to help the people suffering from oppression. What a cruel world.

# Chapter 10

## REWIND

### Desarae's Bedroom

Deshawn jumps up, sweating and hyperventilating. He clutches his chest where he thought he was shot. Desarae reaches up without fully waking up and grabs his shoulder. "Baby, come back to sleep. You gotta look rested for the interview tomorrow."

Deshawn, upon hearing her voice, jumps out the bed and rolls on the floor toward the door, then he stops. Deshawn is sitting up, breathing heavily. He is paralyzed by what he just experienced. Desarae, hardly lifting her face off the pillow, obviously can't be bothered out of how comfortable she is in bed, groggily says, "It was a dream, bae. Come back to sleep. You got that interview in the morning for your book."

Deshawn is still frozen, taking deep and erratic breaths—quick inhale, quiet exhale, quick inhale, quiet exhale, quick inhale. He lays in the bed wide awake, thinking about that crazy dream he just had. It seemed so real. He takes off his shirt. There is blood on the shirt. He checks his body for wounds, but there aren't any. He gets into the bed but stays away from Desarae.

### Deshawn's Home—Next Morning (Interview)

The next morning Deshawn snuck out of Desarae's apartment without waking her up. He decided he didn't want to speak to her anymore. He went home, showered and made sure the place was nice and ready. Deshawn decided to rent an Airbnb for the week instead of inviting anyone to his home. Stacy came with her film crew and set up. They begin the interview.

"Good evening, and welcome to another edition of *The Stacy McGee Show*. As always, I am your host, Stacy McGee. Tonight, we have an incredibly special guest. He is a best-selling author who has previously been listed on the *New York Times* best-seller list, and tonight, he will be discussing his newest book *How to Deal with Death and Missing Your Loved Ones*. We are very honored to have him tonight, Author Deshawn Jones. Mr. Jones, thank you so much for joining us tonight." Says Stacy. Deshawn smiles. "Thank you for having me, always a pleasure." Stacy continued. "So give us a little background on your new book, *How to Deal with Death*."

Deshawn replied. "I wrote this book in hopes of assisting those who are finding it difficult to deal with loss in their own lives by pulling from the experiences of loss I've had in mine. When I began writing, I was going through a lot of traumatic losses myself. I dedicated this book to my mom, dad, grandfather. None of those were easy losses to overcome, but I feel that the best way to deal with death is to focus on life." Stacy curiously asked. "Focus on life to deal with death?" Deshawn replied. "The spirit never dies. To be out of body is to be in the presence of God." Stacy began to dig deeper. "Very interesting perspective, Mr. Jones. I do want to say I am sorry for your losses. And how is your brother?"

Deshawn just stares at the reporter. "He is living his best life." Deshawn answered. He asked to be excused from the interview and they wrapped things up and the reporter and her crew left.

# Chapter 11

## Aftermath

Deshawn is sitting in his living room, staring off into space. He is replaying memories of his brother, Andre, passing and is feeling down. Then suddenly, Deshawn's phone rings. He looks and is astonished to see that it is Andre calling him. He thinks to himself that it must be Londa calling from Andre's number or maybe someone may have his number now. He listens to the phone ring but decides to answer at the last minute.

Deshawn answers hesitantly. "Hello?"

"Man, why you answer the phone like you talking to a ghost or something?" Andre asks on the other line.

Deshawn hangs up the phone quick and runs to the bathroom to throw water on his face. He looks in the mirror in disbelief. "I must be dreaming," he says to himself. He then pinches himself and looks around to see if he is awake. The phone suddenly rings again. Deshawn is now looking at the phone in disbelief. He answers the phone. "Dre?"

Andre replies, "Man, what in the fuck are you smoking, bruh? I need some of that shit right the fuck now, straight up!"

Deshawn mumbles under his breath. "The cancer?"

Andre hears him and says, "Bruh, you and Zack told me to eat the plant and drink that pH water." Deshawn is totally bewildered at this point. Andre continues speaking, "Yeah, ya'll saved a nigga life, man. I won't never forget that shit, the healing is in the herbs."

Deshawn agrees and responds by saying "Facts!" with pure enthusiasm. Deshawn is smiling uncontrollably and is elated at the thought of his brother still alive. It is almost as if he changed reality through his previous dream.

Andre then says, "Listen, man, I know you left the rap game alone, but I think you should manage me. I'm goin' back in, bro, and who else than my celebrity author brother to manager me?"

Deshawn really doesn't want to deal with the rap game anymore but is reluctant to assist his brother being that he thought his brother was dead.

"Meet me at the studio at five p.m. I'm going to record my first single in three years. I want you to be there, Dee," says Andre.

Deshawn replies, "Say less, fam."

Deshawn is puzzled; he stares at the floor, trying to make sense of what is going on. He goes to the bathroom and runs the shower. While in the shower, Deshawn remembers the story of Edgar Cayce, the sleeping prophet. He ponders in his mind, "What if I'm the black Edgar Cayce?" He turns off the shower and dries himself off. He looks in the mirror and is not happy with his body. "Damn, I gotta dad bod wit no kids." He decides to put on his white neighborhood Sotaboy shirt since they are from Sarasota and it's only right to represent. He puts on some jean shorts and all white Js to match. Deshawn makes way to his vehicle, which is a red 2006 Dodge Charger, 5.7 L with the hemi. He can't help but rush to the studio to see his brother.

## In the Studio

Deshawn walks in the studio and greets the engineer. He is met with a big hug by Londa. Andre is in the booth, but he acknowledges his brother, Deshawn. Zack walks in with two bottles of Hennessey and a blunt behind each ear with two more in his mouth. Zack is wearing a flowered pink-and-green button-up shirt with green slacks and brown leather loafers.

"Let's go!" Zack yells.

Deshawn is happy to see Zack and Andre together again. It is like a dream come true—literally. The engineer turns on the beat, and Deshawn is hypnotized by the beat. He remembers all the hours he, Andre, and Zack spent in their homemade studio when they first started rapping.

The engineer plays the beat; it is a survival-type beat with a UK drill base line.

Andre begin his song.

Hook

"After all this time, they still trying to harm us, but I ain't going out. Give me death before dishonor. After all this time, they still trying to harm us, but I ain't going out give me death before dishonor."

Verse

Give me death before dishonor, who gon' die first
Not me, you gon' ride away in the hearse
The big limo to the pearly gates or the trap door
Conversations about beef? I'm 'bout war
I mastered spiritual gifts like a pastor
And I'mma give you what you want
Because you asked for it
It's closing time, deadly blows if I touch 'em
I'm going for mine, it's like death when I rush 'em
I'm a fool for mine, oh, I love the rush, I warned 'em, now deal with definite destruction

Hook

"After all this time, they still trying to harm us, but I ain't going out. Give me death before dishonor. After all this time, they still trying to harm us, but I ain't going out give me death before dishonor."

Everyone is digging the track; it is dope. Andre comes out of the booth, and everyone goes outside to burn while the engineer mixes and masters the track.

Zack says, "Cuz in the booth spitting that lava!" He gives Andre pound.

Deshawn follows up. "Yes, indeed, I see you still got it!"

"You need to get yo ass back in the game too, bro," Andre replies.

"Nah, man, I think I'mma focus on these books 'cause I'm making more money now than I ever did rapping." Deshawn responded.

They finish burning and drinking then go back into the studio to listen to the mastered track. By this time, the producer has arrived and enters through the back door. "Hello, everyone, I'm Mark Sagon," he says. "I produced this track, and my engineer Todd emailed me this track you just did, Dre. This is really good. I have connections with the biggest labels in the world. I think your voice needs to be heard, and I'm willing to offer you a major deal. I can make you a celebrity overnight. What is your stage name?"

"Lunatic," Andre replies. Zack and Deshawn looks at each other.

"I really think you should meet the owner of the record label. He should be here any minute." As soon as he said that, the door opens and in walks ten masked, heavily armed soldiers. They survey the area, and they stand in single file line at the door. In walks a man that stood damn near ten feet tall and is every bit of muscle. His eyes are unearthly as they have a pale haze. Behind him was a man standing 6'3 in his late sixties. They walk over to the table, and the smaller man takes a seat while everyone else just stands in formation.

Everyone was actually shocked silent at their arrival and the fashion in which they arrived. Deshawn really didn't know what was going on, but his spirit was jittery. *Something isn't right about this,* Deshawn thought to himself. He felt like he had woken up from a nightmare only to meet a demon in the flesh. The label was called North Star Records. They had only produced some of the last three decades of multiplatinum recording artist! The label owner was a tall Israeli by the name of Theodore Owens. The studio they were in happened to have another ten studios in the same building. Mr. Owens was there to personally see a few local artist that were making a lot of noise in the area. They were streaming independently, and they recorded in the same studio. The studio was called Wave Central Studios.

In walked a group that called themselves the Muck Boys and two other solo artists. One of them being a tall, slender white boy with red nails. He called himself Li'l Creep. The other solo artist was called Li'l Throwit. The Muck Boys apparently were also going in as solo artists. Their names were Brent "The Sleep God," Boss Black "The Savior," and Six Temptation, a.k.a. "Six." Everyone was really hyped and excited. They were about to have a life-changing deal soon.

The label owner went into a room and each artist went in alone to speak with the owner. Deshawn pulled Andre to the side. "Dre, I think we need to think about this. This is way too soon to sign with a major label. You don't even have a demo recorded. These guys seem weird, bro," Deshawn said.

Andre replied, "I'll be honest, this shit creepy as fuck, bro. But I need to see what they talking about. I'm not trying to just sign a deal right now, but I need to see what kinda money on the table. This might be my big break, I been struggling my whole damn life, shit."

Deshawn, remembering how stubborn his brother was, decided to just have his back and offer advice when he needed it. "Whatever you wanna do, bro," Deshawn says.

Zack was really quiet the whole time, and so was Londa. Zack stood up and walked over to the producer. "Here is my card, you can reach me at this e-mail. If you are interested in signing Lunatic, e-mail the contract to review with his lawyers and let's set up a meeting. We are leaving now."

The producer looked shocked. "Umm, OK, How about we meet up in two weeks? I am hosting a mansion party in LA. Your rooms are already paid for at the Casa Del Mar," he said. "There will be several celebrities there, and we will play your song a few times."

Andre couldn't pass on that offer. "See you there!" Andre said. And he shook hands with the producer.

Deshawn, Andre, Zack, and Londa left the studio, and they agreed to all meet at Deshawn's crib.

## At Deshawn's Place

Everyone showed up at Deshawn's place around the same time. Deshawn pulled out an ounce of White Runtz and placed it on the coffee table. Everyone rolled up a solo blunt and poured their own troubles. Deshawn broke the silence. "So what we doing, Dre?"

Andre replied, "We going back to Cali, Cali, Cali." Everyone laughed.

Zack chimed in, "Listen, man, I'm coming, all three of us are going. This shit ain't no joke, these people are evil. The whole industry is satanic. Ya'll sure ya'll tryna be in LA and Holly Weird? I ain't tryna be nobody's sacrifice!"

Deshawn agreed, "Shiit, me either! But it's money on the table. We gotta walk light and make sure we have Dre's back."

Andre also spoke up, "We got this fa sho."

Deshawn started booking airline tickets. "We need to double-check and make sure we are good at the hotel. I wonder how long the rooms are booked for? That will let us know what type of business they are trying to conduct," Deshawn said. Everyone agreed with Deshawn. All three were on the same page. This was going to be a power move to advance to the next level if done right. However, they all knew the behind-the-scene dangers that were associated with hip-hop.

## Later that Night

Deshawn was lying alone that night after burning a spliff. He laid there trying to make sense of everything that's going on. He suddenly remembered a prayer he said when he was around eighteen. He asked the Lord to use him in the battle against good and evil. As he was in deep thought, Deshawn began dosing off. Deshawn opened his eyes because he felt a presence in the room! He looked up, and low and behold, there was a shadow figure of a man standing directly over Deshawn. Deshawn tried to get up, but he was paralyzed. He tried to scream, but nothing would come out. Deshawn looked over to his right, and he saw himself walking out of the room! In some type of way, the being had superior power over Deshawn. When Deshawn looked at its face, he saw it did not have one. It was like a complete shadow in 3D. Deshawn knew that if his body walked away from that room, something bad would happen.

"Jesus, help me!" he cried out in his mind. And in that instance, a shining light appeared at the foot of the bed! The shadow being vanished as if it were afraid. The light was so bright Deshawn could not really look at it. Inside the light, it looked like the figure of a man that stood so tall Deshawn couldn't see past his knees. Deshawn noticed his skin was shining like polished brass. Suddenly, Deshawn heard a voice.

"Deshawn," the voice said. It called Deshawn's name once, then it faded away, as if it were some type of portal. Deshawn jumped up, and he looked around. He knew to call on the Son of God in a time like that. He was taught that by his grandfather and his grandmother at an early age. Who knew that spirits and other dimensions really existed? More importantly, they respected the Most High and his Son.

"Thank you, Lord, for saving me. In the name of Jesus. Amen," Deshawn prayed. Deshawn felt at peace. The voice did not scare him so that means it was of God. Deshawn was starting to realize that something was changing within himself. It's almost as if his reality wasn't real. *From losing Andre to waking up and going to the studio recording music and now going to a celebrity mansion party is crazy,* Deshawn thought to himself. All he could think about was Edgar Cayce. Deshawn then knew that he had to get to Virginia Beach, Virginia. The Edgar Cayce library might give him some answers. Deshawn said his prayers and went to sleep.

## The Dream

As Deshawn slept, he began to dream. He was walking along the mountainside near an ocean. The water was crashing on the rocks so much that it was splashing on Deshawn. Deshawn followed a row of steps leading to a huge white mansion. Deshawn looked up, and low and behold, he saw angels with wings flying in the sky. Deshawn kept walking to the mansion. He went to the door, and someone was there waiting for him. It was a woman in the form of Oprah Winfrey. Perhaps a doppelganger of some sort. She invited Deshawn inside. They walked up what Deshawn felt were five flights of stairs or more. She took Deshawn to the rooftop, and Deshawn saw people with gliders on their back, running and jumping off the roof of the mansion. They were soaring above the water under the covering of the sun's rays. Deshawn then realized those were not angels. He realized that heaven on earth wasn't what it was cracked up to be. "Why gain the riches but loose your soul in the process?" he asked himself. Suddenly, Deshawn opened his eyes to the sound of his alarm on his cell phone. It was four hours until his flight departure. He got up and showered and prepared to meet Zack and Andre at the airport.

# Chapter 12

## TEMPTATION

Everyone met at the airport. While waiting, Zack said, "I hope nan one of ya'll brought anything red or blue!"

Andre replied. "Straight up, ha ha."

Deshawn laughed and said, "I'm trying to make it home without a toe tag."

They all boarded the plane. Once they arrived to the airport in LA, they rented an all-black 2020 Dodge Hellcat. They drove to the hotel to check in and get settled. The room was immaculate. It had three bedrooms; it was like a mini mansion.

Everybody got cleaned up and headed out. It was 9:00 p.m. in Cali. Zack had an idea. "So what are we going to call ourselves? I mean, we are the clique," he said.

"I like 360 Rebels," Andre added, as if he had already gave it some thought.

"I like that," Deshawn exclaimed. They put the address in the GPS and made their way to the mansion party.

### The Mansion Party

The GPS led them to a huge mansion on top of the hills. They arrived to a huge white gate. "That mansion has to be sitting on 100 acres at least," Andre stated. At the gate were about twenty security guards. There were five on the outside and fifteen on the inside. They were checking people off the list before they were allowed to go through the gate. Zack, Deshawn, and Andre were on the list, so they went through the gate and drove until they were met by a security guard directing cars. They were directed to a place to park. They got out and walked up to the mansion. They were escorted inside to the party. There were about 200 to 300 people inside the mansion, and about 150 people gathered outside. It was a cool night at 65 degrees, and Hollywood's finest came out to party. The guys saw some of their favorite artist, actors, models, rappers, singers, and television host all in the same place. They decided to walk around and act as if this were nothing new to them.

Zack yelled over the music to Andre, "Look at all this rich pussy walking round."

Andre yelled back, "Here, kitty, kitty!" They both laughed. Deshawn was quiet and more observant of his surroundings. He chose not to drink and to stay on point. All three of them wore boots. They were able to sneak their pistols in past security.

"We gotta make sure we don't get separated," Deshawn said. Zack and Andre agreed with him. This mansion was humongous. The ceiling was at least twenty feet high. The house had three stories with over twenty rooms. They stopped for a minute to get drinks.

Andre ordered the drinks. "Let me get six shots of Patrón and lemon," he said. The bartender poured them six shots, and Deshawn tipped her twenty bucks. The bartender looked at the tip and looked at Deshawn with a frown. Deshawn looked at the bartender and smiled. "Thanks, baby cheeks," he said jokingly. He, Zack, and Andre made a toast before taking shots. "We riiich, biiiiiiiitch!" Zack exclaimed. They all took back a shot. As soon as the cups touched the bar, they took back the second shot in sync.

"Whoooaaa!" Deshawn exclaimed. Right there at the corner of the bar was a bowl of pills. People were just grabbing them and popping them.

They kept walking through the mansion party until they came to a big den type of room. "Yo, what the fuck is this?!" Deshawn burst out. There was about twenty people lying on a large padded floor. They were all cuddling up with one another. Men were spooning other men, women were spooning with other women, and men and women were cuddled up with one another.

Deshawn quickly walked past that situation. "Man, did ya'll see that shit?" Deshawn asked Zack and Andre. No one responded. Deshawn turned around to see Zack and Andre was missing. He looked into the crowd, and there was Zack and Andre, side by side dancing with two big-bootied women. Deshawn could look and tell that his cousin and his brother were high as hell off more than weed. Deshawn could see they had taken a few pills. "I knew it, fucking party animals. I might as well look around," Deshawn said to himself.

He walked past another room, and the door was cracked. Deshawn stopped because he heard a familiar voice. "Going platinum, and I get a few parts in some box office hits?" Then another masculine voice said, "Yes." Deshawn heard that familiar voice again. "OK, I'll do it." Deshawn looked around to see who was looking. He then peeped through the opening in the door. He saw the producer

Mark Sagon standing up, and the rapper Li'l Creep was giving him a blow job! Deshawn backed away from the door, looked around to see if anyone saw him, and walked away. *That was disgusting,* Deshawn thought to himself. He thought about his brother Andre. He knew that it wasn't in his brother's best interest to be a part of this record label. Deshawn hurried to go find Andre and Zack.

As he looked for Zack, he walked past a room that sounded like twenty people were having an orgy in it. Deshawn was troubled in his spirit. As he looked around the mansion, he could see what looked like small shadow spirits moving around faster than the blink of an eye. Deshawn was ready to go.

He located Andre and Zack over by the DJ. By this time, there were about eight women surrounding them, dancing. Booty was rocking everywhere. Zack and Andre was on 'em. I mean, they were on those women like a frankfurter sliding in and out a hotdog bun. Deshawn didn't want to break up their fun. Suddenly, Deshawn realized what was going on. The women were separating Zack and Andre. Four women grabbed Zack, and four grabbed Andre. The women split the two of them up by dancing on them and pulling them in different directions. Deshawn watched which room the ladies dragged Zack into. And he witnessed the ladies stop with Andre, and one came up behind him. She grabbed his butt. Andre turned around, and she blew a powdery substance from her hand into his face. She then whispered something in his ear. Andre's demeanor changed suddenly once Deshawn inhaled it. They then walked into a room, and Deshawn ran toward them before they went into the room. Deshawn immediately knew that they had used the Columbian drug. That drug turns you into a zombie for hours, and the victim will do whatever you tell them.

"Oh hell nah!" Deshawn yelled as he kicked the door down before it closed. Inside the room were four white guys with a camera setup. Two of them were barely dressed. Deshawn could tell it was a setup for his brother. He grabbed Andre's arm and said to him, "Come with me, Andre, and don't listen to nobody but me!"

Andre nodded. "OK," he said with a blank stare.

"If anyone try to stop us, knock they bitch ass the fuck out! Let's get Zack and get the fuck outta here, now!"

"OK," Andre replied.

Everyone just stopped and looked at Deshawn grab Zack and leave. No one said anything. They all had this sadistic smile on their face. Deshawn ran to the room where Zack was at and kicked down the door! And there was Zack, lying on the bed motionless while one female was straddling his midsection, one was holding his feet, and the larger one was sitting on his face. Deshawn ran over and pushed the big girl to the floor. He heard a large thump, and the other girls ran out the room. Zack took a huge breath and opened his eyes and looked around. He saw Deshawn standing over him, slapping the shit out his face. He finally came to and felt the sting of the next slap from Deshawn.

"Awwwwww, shit! You motherfucker!" Zack yelled as he grabbed his face and sat upward. "I'm 'bout to kick your motherfucking ass, Dee!" He looked down. "Damn, where my pants at?"

Deshawn threw him his pants. "We getting the fuck outta here, now!"

Zack put on his pants and looked at Andre. Andre was staring off in space. "Bro, you looked fucked up," Zack said. They left the room and made their way out the door. "Man, what in the fuck just happened?" Zack asked.

"Yo ass almost died in there with them chicks. Andre got that Colombian drug blown in his face, and they almost initiated his ass," Deshawn said.

"Colombian drug?" Andre mumbled.

"Sounds like he coming around," Deshawn said.

They made their way to the car and got in. "Both of ya'll owe me big time!"

Andre spoke up, "I remembered going to smash these chicks. Everything else is hazy, like a dream."

Zack also spoke up. "Yeah, man, I remember going in the room, and I was lying down, and one chick took my pants off and started deep throating it, then suddenly, everything went dark. I looked up, and you slapped me, bitch." He then playfully slaps Deshawn while he was driving back to the hotel.

"Stop playing, man, yo ass almost got killed by a fat ass, literally. You was in there getting smothered with ya legs twitching and all," said Deshawn while shaking his head.

Zack replied, "Damn, that sounds like the perfect way to go!" Then he released the most sinister laugh from deep within. "Pwhooohahahahha!" Andre, fully alert now, began laughing too.

"Ohhhhh, you laughing, bruh?!" Deshawn snapped. "Bro, they blew that Columbian drug in your face and turned you into a zombie. They took you in a room, and it was a bunch of white old men in there about to lick and roll you like a natural leaf!" Deshawn yelled to Andre. Andre and Zack looked at each other. Neither one was willing to admit what happened, but they were both grateful Deshawn was alert.

## At the Hotel

They get to the hotel and headed to the room. Zack said, "I don't know about ya'll, but I'm not trying to stay in LA tonight. This whole shit just freaked me out."

The guys grabbed their luggage and walked out in two minutes. They checked out of the hotel, loaded up the car, and hopped in the car. Deshawned looked up and was startled to see Agent Nueman and Agent Holdman walking past his car.

Then the feeling of fear suddenly turned into anger, and Deshawn grabbed his .40 Glock and cocked it back. Upon hearing the sound of a Deshawn's gun cocking back, Andre, within a flash, pulled out his 9 mm Glock and Zack pulled out his Keltech P32. Andre looked at Deshawn and Zack, then looked around to see why Deshawn reacted the way he did. He saw the two agents walking toward the car. Everybody was in position, but the guns were out of sight. Deshawn saw them looking into the car as they approached.

"Can I help you," he asked.

Agent Nueman replied, "We are with the label. We are just checking to the make sure things are OK."

"Things are great! You guys have a nice day, and thank you very much for all that you do," Deshawn said with a fake smile as he pulled off.

Agent Holdman shouts to Deshawn. "Wait! Do you remember me?" He points two fingers at Deshawn in the form of a gun and smiles. "Oh, no, that had to be a different assignment." He looks at Deshawn sideways and removes his glasses to really get a good luck at Deshawn. "Good day to you," he says without cracking a smile.

Deshawn pulls off in deep thought. The agents were not a dream. Deshawn was at a lost for words so much he could not drive. "I need somebody to drive," said Deshawn as he pulled over and got in the back seat. Zack jumped in the front seat. "What's wrong, cuz?" he asked Deshawn.

"If I tell ya'll this shit, promise me you won't think I'm crazy," Deshawn said.

"I can't do that," Andre replied while laughing.

"I've been having these weird dreams lately. But the thing about it is, I really think it's real. I can't explain it. Those two agents tried to kill me in this dream I had a few weeks ago," Deshawn expressed.

Andre asked him, "Why would they try to kill you?"

Deshawn replied, "Because, Zack and I released the cure to cancer after you died from it."

Zack chimed in, "That's heavy."

There was a silence, and then Andre spoke up. "I dreamt that I died from cancer … I stopped smoking cigarettes and Black & Milds two weeks ago."

Zack replied, "I dreamt that Deshawn was robbed at a barbershop and killed. Well, that's what the news said."

"Well, in my dream, it wasn't a robbery. Those two agents shot at me, but Desarae killed me in my dream. She was an undercover FBI agent. After seeing those two devils, I know God is trying to tell me something. I gotta figure it out. I'm going to the Cayce center in VA to speak with someone after we get back."

Andre looked at his phone as he just received an IG message. "Well, don't go just yet. I just got offer to feature on a song. I said I want $10k, and he just sent it via Cash app. Let's pull up to Chicago. I got a rack fa both of ya'll," he said.

Deshawn and Zack both agreed to head there with Andre. "Not bad for an independent artist," said Zack while giving Andre pound. They turned up the music and took turns driving to Chicago. The radio was playing. "And the number 1 song on the Billboard 100—'Pop a Perc' by Li'l Creep!!" Everyone in the car looked at one another.

# Chapter 13

## HERE COMES THE WAR

They pulled up to the studio. They walk through the door and went to the secretary. "I'm here to record with D.O.A. Big Bang. Tell 'em it's Lunatic." The secretary picked up her cell and called Big Bang. "Bang, the Lunatic hea," she said in the most ratchet way. The studio room opened, and the room was filled with weed smoke. Big Bang came out with five goons to greet everyone. Bang was five foot nine; he was 235 lb. of solid muscle.

"What up, Lunatic? I see you a real one. You came right here as soon as I sent the bread. I can respect any nigga that understands the seriousness of not playing wit a nigga money. Thanks for coming!"

Andre replied, "I appreciate you considering me for this song and for sending everything up front. When I saw that, I knew you was not fucking around. So I'm here, let's work."

They went into the recording room, and there were ten other dudes in there. They all had guns on them. Some handguns had thirty-round drums while others had extended clips. They had AK-47s and ARs too.

Big Bang turned on a beat that was pure fire. It was more of a UK drill baseline. It had death bells ringing and a sample of a woman crying. Andre was impressed with the beat. "This shit hard as fuck," said Andre.

"Yessah, I'm glad you rockin' wit it," responded Big Bang. "Check out the hook," said Bang.

"I'm 'bout to stand over a nigga and shoot him his face,

I got money to get so I took 'em on a race,

When them crackers caught me,

I fucked around and beat the case,

Fired up that J Murder pack and went and pissed on his grave."

He finished the hook then turned down the music and looked at Andre. "I just need eight to twelve bars from you. We riding on the Ops on this shit."

Deshawn could look at Andre and see what he was thinking. He truly wasn't expecting the song to be a direct diss to a dead man that he didn't even know. However, he was in a position where this could go left quick fast and in a hurry. "Aight bet" is the only thing Andre said. "Turn the mic on, I'm going in," he added.

Andre walked in the booth without anything wrote. "Is he going to freestyle?" Zack asked Deshawn.

"I guess so," replied Deshawn. Andre put on the headphones. They turned on the beat, and he begin freestyling.

"I ain't got shit to say, I let my gun do the talking, Blaaat,

Enter ya chest, exit ya back,

Now release the demon,

I should pop ya dad for releasing that semen,

Snitch ass Op, you a rat,

I paid ya mans two racks to let me in through the back,

You don't really wanna start it with this,

Throw me the ball, dog, and I bet I don't fumble,

Hit the club, I'm high,

Roll with thunder,

I'm a lion in the jungle, and I'm cold with hunger.

See, Joshua fought the battles over Jericho, and the walls came tumbling down,

I rep the Sota now there we go, a real nigga, and I won't back down."

As Andre was rapping his verse, a person was filming him for footage. Andre showed the gun and holster on his hip. Andre came out the booth, and the room seemed to have a more respective energy vibe.

"Man, that was pure fire!" said Bang. "How long ya'll boys in town?"

"We in and out. I just stopped by to see you on this business, and we headed out now," Andre replied.

"OK, OK, well, if you in town tonight, hit me up. We in VIP at the Club Shiznit."

Andre replied, "Aight bet." Andre gave Bang dap, then he, Zack, and Deshawn walked out and went to the car. All three got in the car.

"I was trying to get the hell outta there," said Andre. "I feel that, I saw the dudes in there with their cell phones out while ya'll in there dissing people 'n' shit."

Zack chimed in. "They was probably giving their ops the location," said Zack.

As they prepared to pull off, they looked up and saw a black van with dark, black tints pull up to the side of the studio. There were four brothers standing outside smoking a blunt. They were a part of Big Bang's gang. Deshawn looked closely, and he told Zack and Andre to get down as he saw Agent Nueman roll down the windows and start shooting at the guys outside the studio. There was three other agents with Nueman, and they let off fifty rounds into the studio, killing all four men that was standing outside. Big Bang and some of the guys from inside came around back and returned fire at the black van. The van sped off while someone screamed from the van, "Z block muhfuka, ya'll ain't shit!"

The van got away. No one saw the agents but Deshawn. Andre, Zack, and Deshawn got out the car to go check on the guys at the studio. "Somebody call an ambulance!" someone yelled.

"We heard the gunshots and saw a black van pulling off," said Andre to Bang. "Ya'll might wanna get up outta here."

"It's drill time," said Bang. It just so happened that the gang's block they were beefing with was less than five minutes away. Three people from Bang's clique stepped up. It was two dudes and a female. The girl had to be like seventeen years old. Come to find out she was their top assassin. They called her Jane DOE. Jane was from the same hood as everyone else, and she was a known shooter. She caught her first body when she was thirteen. She was a good girl in school, but the environment will change you. Her favorite cousin was shot in the head five times and killed while standing outside of a party by Z block members. He was only eleven years old. Six months later, they shot and killed her cousin Justin at a bus stop. Her uncle was an OG, and he taught her how to kill and get away with it. Once she was ready for target practice, the members would drive over to a rival gang's block and shoot at them, then ride off. Jane did not miss on her first mission. She had pinpoint accuracy as she let of nine shots, hitting and killing two opps as they ran for their lives.

She stood about five foot five and weighed around 135. Jane was very beautiful. She was sexy in every aspect. Deshawn just stared at her in awe as she hopped in the all-black Charger with three other members, with guns loaded. The car peeled off. Just as she left, the ambulance and sirens could be heard getting closer. Bang didn't want to be seen by the police, so he hopped in the car with Zack, Andre, and Deshawn. The other members followed, leaving four members behind to look after the wounded gang members.

Bang directed Deshawn to pull in the area where they lived in Parkside Gardens. As everyone stood outside, you could hear gunshots going off in the distance. It sounded like over twenty shots rang out. Within five minutes of hearing the gunshots, you could see the Charger speeding past, and everyone hopped out. They gave the keys to a base head named Ottis, and he drove the car to the chop shop. Jane and the three goons walked up, laughing and mimicking the people whom they just murdered.

"That li'l nigga was sitting there, smoking a blunt. Fucked around and got smoked like a blunt! Eye for eye, bitch, we up!" said Jane. Everyone agreed. She rolled up and passed the blunt to Bang. Bang gave her $5,000 for making a hit on the opps. She kept two thousand and gave her comrades the rest. Bang started smoking the blunt and went live on his social media. He hit the blunt a few times and waited until he had fifty viewers.

"We smoking dat Bo Bo pack, bitch!" He put the camera on Jane and the other killers. They all started repping their set and throwing up signs. By then, Deshawn, Zack, and Andre were in the car. "Bang, you be safe out here, stay in touch," Andre said to Bang.

"10-4, we got people all over the state. This D.O.A. gang shit my nigga. If you ever need us, we gon' pull up," replied Bang.

"Bet that up, brother," Andre replied.

Deshawn intervened. "But I have a question to ask you before I leave. Why all the dissing dead people on music, bruh? And why are you still here? This shit seems like an endless cycle to me. They kill ya'll, ya'll kill them."

Bang thought about responding to Deshawn. "They killed my brother, my cousin, and three of my close friends. They stood over my nigga and dumped twelve bullets in his face and body. After that, I hear all these songs and videos about my cousin. He was doing positive shit. They shot him over fifteen times! He was on his way to football practice! He ain't wanna be involved in this gang shit. None of us do. Ain't no way I'mma sit back and let them disrespect my people. Plus, the hood and family hurting, so I gotta represent for folks nem, ya feel me?!" Bang expressed with anger and hurt.

Deshawn understood and gave Bang dap. "Thanks for helping me understand," said Deshawn. Bang nodded his head toward Deshawn. Everybody went their separate ways.

Andre, Zack, and Deshawn began driving back to Sarasota, Florida. "Guys, I gotta tell ya'll something. I saw that same white dude from the hotel at the studio. He was driving the van, and he was shooting out the window. He was dressed in regular clothes too," stated Deshawn as they were driving down I75 past Tallahassee, Florida.

"How in the hell would he be in the same place as us twice in a row, and on top of that, in the hood shooting niggas with other niggas? That don't make no damn sense," Andre replied.

"Unless he's a clone that's been duplicated for evil, diabolical purposes. Pwhoohahahahaha!" Zack blurted out.

"I just feel like it's something wrong in the world, and I need to help fix it. I feel like I was chosen to do something about it," Deshawn stated. They didn't say much on the way home. Everybody was processing what transpired over the week.

# Chapter 14

## The Awakening

The next morning, Deshawn decided to spend some time alone. He checked his social media and noticed the song with his brother and Bang was trending. He had mixed emotions about that. Deshawn was starting to lose touch of what was reality and what wasn't. He really felt like his first dream really did happen. He could still feel the emotions behind it. And now he was seeing people that were in his dream face-to-face.

Deshawn laid down to take a nap. He opened his eyes and sat up. He looked around and couldn't believe his eyes. He saw his body lying there, sleeping.

"I must be dead!" Deshawn said aloud. Suddenly, there was this terrifying ghostly shriek. Paralyzing fear overcame Deshawn. It was a sound that came straight from the depths of hell itself. Deshawn felt like he could do anything he put his mind to in the state he was in. He walked to the wall, looked at it, and walked right through it. *Oh now, that was raw,* he said to himself. Deshawn was looking around for whatever made that sound he heard earlier. He looked up at the sky and thought to himself. "I can fly." And suddenly he began floating. He willed himself higher and thought, *Faster.* He moved as fast as lighting high above the world. He could go and do anything he thought about. Then he thought about his mother and father. As soon as he thought about them, he could feel them. He heard his mother's voice come from the clouds. "Get back to your body before he gets to it!" she said.

Deshawn couldn't believe his mom was there too. He thought to get back to his body, and within a blink of an eye, he was there with his body. And there, standing between Deshawn and his body, was the demon Baphomet that reigned over the entertainment industry. It stood about fifteen feet tall. He had the head of a goat with red bloodshot eyes. His horns were six feet apart. His body was that of a man, except it had a woman's breast. To Deshawn's surprise, it spoke to him in a deep thunderous voice. "Deshawn, join me and I will give you all your heart desires," said the Baphomet.

"No thank you, devil man. I'm Gucci," Deshawn replied.

"Very well then," said the Baphomet. Deshawn's lack of fear and respect angered Baphomet. He placed his index finger on the forehead of Deshawn's sleeping physical body. Deshawn's physical body began to shake as he stopped breathing. Deshawn knew immediately that Baphomet was going to keep him there, which meant he was about to die on the earthly material dimension in which his physical body lay helpless.

Once again, fear gripped the mind of Deshawn as he saw this happening. He cried out, "Yahshua, help me, please!" As soon as he cried out unto the Son of the Most High God, a brilliant light appeared. The look of fear overcame Baphomet, and it moved with the speed of lighting into a black portal that opened in the kitchen. Deshawn jumped up out of his sleep, looking around.

"Wow, these dreams are getting realer and realer," Deshawn said to himself. He put on his jogging clothes and went to the park for a jog. As Deshawn was jogging through the park, he noticed someone following him. He sped up, and the person sped up also. Deshawn wasn't in great shape, and his jog slowed down to a speed walk. He then sat down on the park bench to catch his breath. Deshawn realized that it had been a woman following him. She actually sat down next to Deshawn on the bench.

*Wow,* Deshawn thought to himself. She was very well put together. She was tall in stature, standing about six foot one and must weigh 220 pounds. She was wearing all-black jogging pants, all-black Nikes, and an all-black hoodie.

"Hello, Deshawn," she said. Deshawn was shocked at first, but then his arrogance kicked in. Perhaps she recognized him as being an author.

"Hello, I'm sorry, I didn't get your name," Deshawn replied.

"I'm Sarai." She smiled as she introduced herself.

"So how do you know who I am?" Deshawn asked.

"I've been waiting for you," Sarai replied.

"OK, you've been here at the park waiting for me?" Deshawn replied.

"No, Deshawn," Sarai answered. "I've been waiting for you to wake up. You've been dreaming your whole life. But recently, you been waking up. But after you wake, you are doing all you can to go back to sleep."

"OK, you have my attention," Deshawn replied.

"Deshawn, you have a choice: there is a war waging in the spiritual realm. This war will manifest into the physical realm, thus springing forth the Antichrist. I think you met one of his generals the other day, correct?" said Sarai.

Deshawn was amazed and curious. "How do you know all of this? How do you know what I am going through?" Deshawn asked.

"All your life, you have had this feeling inside. You feel that you are not normal, you feel as if you are a superhero. You feel like there is something major that you were born to do. You feel like you have a purpose. You tend to follow your feelings more so than what you are taught or told. You see, Deshawn, reality has been manipulated. The adversary has this world in a state of false reality. Which is why the average man uses 10 to 12 percent of his brain," said Sarai.

"So in other words, my life is a simulation?" Deshawn asked.

"Deshawn, I can show you how to let your mind be free," Sarai stated.

"And how can you do that? Can you help me understand what's going on with me?" Deshawn asked.

"I can only show you the truth," Sarai replied.

"And how do you know you can show me the truth, and why should I believe in what you deem as truth?" Deshawn questioned.

"I have been dreaming about you, Deshawn, since I as twelve. I just never knew what it meant until I began to astral travel."

Deshawn was caught between wanting to flirt and take her serious. "And what were your dreams about?" Deshawn asked with a smirk.

Sarai looked at Deshawn with the deepest affection. "I dreamed that Yahshua chose you to prepare the Hebrew Israelites for his second coming. He will give you power that only your mind can handle, although everyone is capable of achieving that power. However, self-doubt is your biggest obstacle. Once you believe, you will have access to over 80 percent of your brain. Then you will be able to battle with the dragon families."

Deshawn's mouth dropped. "Battle? Dragon families?" asked Deshawn.

Sarai could see that Deshawn was about to get up and walk away. She took him by his right hand. "If I tell you something about yourself that only you know, would you believe me and allow me to help you master your abilities?"

Deshawn became a little at ease with the feeling of her touch. Her hand possessed the softest skin that Deshawn had ever felt. It was warm and soothing, as if she were talking with her touch. Deshawn accepted her challenge. "OK, go for it," he said.

"You have a lump in the middle of your right hand." She flipped over Deshawn's hand and rubbed his palm were the lump was located.

Deshawn was impressed. "OK, I'm in, you got me with that one. Although you already had me when you mentioned that thing that attacked me in my dream. So now what?" he asked.

"We need to go somewhere that is safe, comfortable, and quiet."

Deshawn smiled. "That sounds like home," he replied.

Sarai looked at Deshawn and smiled. "Somehow, I knew you were going to say that."

Deshawn laughed as he stood up. "Do you need a lift? It would be my honor to give you a ride," offered Deshawn.

Sarai smiled. "No, thank you, I have my own transportation. I will meet you there," she replied.

"Do you need my address?" Deshawn turned around to face her, but she was gone.


## Deshawn's Place

Deshawn pulled up in his driveway and looked around but did not see Sarai's car. He was slightly disappointed, but as he walked to the front door, he saw Sarai was there waiting for him. Deshawn was truly shocked. Deshawn realized that there was something very different and special about Sarai.

They entered Deshawn's condo and sat on the sofa. "What now?" Deshawn asked.

Sarai replied, "The mind is the portal to the nine dimensions. We ask through prayer, but we receive the answer through meditation. Now repeat after me. Heavenly Father, in the name of Yahshua, please send your angels to watch over our souls and guide and protect our spirits to the Akashic records, amen. Now, Deshawn, I want you to concentrate on your true self. Close your eyes, tell yourself that your spirit and soul are separate. Tell yourself that you have the ability to leave and come back to your soul. Now breathe and focus on your breath."

Deshawn followed her every word, and he began to feel himself float as if he were weightless. "Do not panic, for the spirit of God is with you," said Sarai. Deshawn could hear her voice still. The light got brighter and brighter. The light was really a living angel. The light morphed into a twelve-foot-tall man-like being. It had wings that measured maybe a twenty-foot wingspan. He had polished copper-tone skin that glowed as if a light were embedded inside the angel of the Lord. He wore a white robe as he appeared before Deshawn.

Deshawn was also joined by Sarai in the spirit realm. She also had a glow to her aura in this realm. She took Deshawn by the hand and said to the angel, "Please show him what he needs to see." And suddenly, everything around Deshawn materialized, and they were standing in the corner of a dark room. Inside that room were six priests dressed in all-black robes with hoods attached. They were standing in a circle surrounding a table that contained a fifty-six-inch wide-screen monitor. On that monitor was the music page of Li'l Creep. The page contained his picture and his new album. The album was titled *Shadow God*. The evil priest were chanting and casting spells on the music. Deshawn and Sarai could see dark shadow spirits flow into the computer. The shadow demons just materialized. They moved so fast that all Deshawn saw were black streaks.

Suddenly, they were in a different setting. There was a kid listening to Li'l Creep on his Bluetooth speaker. He began shooting up heroin. The shadow spirits were flowing from the stereo to the middle of his head, right between the eyes. They were taking control of his mind, and they entered his mind through the music. The boy had to be around fourteen. His eyes became black, and he reached inside of his backpack and pulled out a 9 mm handgun. He walked outside and shot someone at point-blank range.

They didn't flew as if they were moving as fast as light to the North Pole and into the hollow earth to Gehana. This place was more like a waiting area. People there had hope as they waited for judgment. It was actually beautiful and very peaceful. There was a wide river, trees, and the sun; and temperature was perfect. Children played while adults laughed and talked. These were called the Neutrals.

Next, they went to Limbo, where the unbaptized babies and many others who did not accept Christ were. In the first circle of hell, there were a lot of former rulers and kings, as they floated in a dark cloud full of scorpion-type bees stinging them with poison over and over. In the second circle, there were souls that were wrought with lust. Deshawn closed his eyes as they descended farther into hell, past lakes with souls fighting one another and levels were sodomites and other tortured souls burned in lakes of fire. Other souls were being devoured by gigantic demons with the heads of animals. They went to the last level of hell were Deshawn saw Satan himself. He was a giant ugly beast with three faces. All faces had a different expression of pure evil. He was in chains, relentlessly clawing the back of Judas.

The angel flew them out of that place to the living room were Deshawn and Sarai's bodies lay. Their souls became one with their body, and they woke up. Deshawn looked over at Sarai, and then he looked around the room. He was in disbelief at what he just saw. All he could do was just stare at Sarai, and she stared back.

# Chapter 15

## WAR

The Next Day

Deshawn was awakened at 8:00 a.m. by a knock on the door. He looked at the security camera, and he could see it was his cousin Zack.

"Man, what hell you up so early for?" Deshawn asked Zack.

"Have you been living under a rock the last two days, cuz?" Zack asked Deshawn.

"What's going on?" Deshawn asked curiously.

Zack looked Deshawn in the eyes and replied, "That damn song that Andre did, man. I know he got paid, but I knew that was a bad move. Now these dudes that Bang nem beefin' wit' wanna get back. They dropped a song dissing Andre and Bang, and they talm 'bout ain't nowhere safe. They shot Bang last night, cuz. But I heard Bang hit like three of 'em, and he managed to get away. Let off three and hit three. But this is the thing, they feel like Andre shouldn't have been on that song dissin' they dead homies. In other words, these motherfuckers trying to do more than just rap my nigga!"

Deshawn looked at Zack and began thinking. "I have to tell you something. You not going to believe this, man," said Deshawn.

"Try me," Zack responded.

"I met this woman in the park, and she knew who I was. She actually knew about my ability. We came here, and she taught me to meditate and focus to a point where I was traveling to other dimensions. I can't quite understand how things change when I wake up, however. But her and I will probably see each other again today. I guess I'm in training," Deshawn stated.

"Sooo in other words, you are the next black hero?" Zack asked sarcastically.

"I'm serious man!" Deshawn exclaimed.

"I believe you, cuz. So you, you need to figure out how you use this ability because we are about to go to war?"

"War? What is it good for, man?" Deshawn asked Zack.

"Absolutely nothing. But, ummm. We have a problem here. I already called Andre. He should be here any minute," said Zack. Deshawn replied. At that moment, Andre was pulling up outside. Andre walked in and spoke to the guys.

"Wat up fellas?" Andre asked.

"What you plan on doing about this rap beef? They already shot Bang, and they not sure if he gon' make it," exclaimed Zack.

Andre fired up a blunt. "We not gon' do shit, but keep moving. These niggas is all talk, man. And Bang is way up there, and they got shit going on bigger than rap. I did a song, I ain't diss they folk. So if any of them dudes run up on me, I'mma buss they ass. Simple as that," Andre said very calmly.

Deshawn knew his brother, and he knew that he wasn't worried. He also knew that his brother can be very dangerous when in battle mode. "Anyways, I'm going shopping. Are ya'll coming or what? Then I'm going to Siesta Key to have some drinks on the beach like a real boss," said Andre.

"I'm in," said Zack.

"I am too, but I have to meet up with you all. I have company coming over shortly, and I must get cleaned up," said Deshawn.

Zack and Andre left while Deshawn locked the door and went and showered. He couldn't help but think about the things he saw when descending to hell. All the tortured souls that lived a life without God, all the souls that were not baptized and the ones that did not accept the Messiah were all there. Deshawn wondered how much of his ability he had access to. Deshawn got out of the shower, and he heard a knock at the door. He began to ask, "Who is—" but the visitor replied, "Sarai."

Before Deshawn could say "Come in," she appeared right in front of him. Deshawn was startled. "How did you do that?!" he asked.

Sarai replied, "I have abilities like you. Your first real test is coming up, Deshawn. They are coming for you, they know who you are. They have direct contact with the fallen one."

Deshawn needed to understand his abilities more. "How do I use my abilities?" he asked Sarai.

She looked him in his eyes with love, and she replied, "You have to believe, and just do it."

Deshawn gave this thought, and he decided to put himself to the test on the spot. "So if I believe I can walk through this door, I can do it, huh?" Deshawn asked while staring at the closed room door. Sarai didn't say anything. She just watched Deshawn and tried not to laugh. Deshawn took a deep breath and walked into the door. There was a loud thud as the door halted his forward progress. However, Deshawn's spirit kept walking into the next room. He turned around, happy and smiling, only to see through the door and witness his lifeless body falling to the ground. In this state, it was as if everything were slowed down in the flesh and material realm. He saw Sarai reaching toward his body in slow motion, as if she were attempting to catch Deshawn from hitting the ground. Deshawn decided to go back into his body, and faster than the blink of an eye, he was catching himself from falling. He turned around and hugged Sarai as soon as she got off the chair to catch his body. Sarai was shocked that Deshawn was able to perform this feat.

"How did you do that?" she asked him.

"I don't know," Deshawn responded.

Sarai was amazed. She looked at Deshawn with excitement, then she realized he was still hugging her. She gently pushed him away, but she took him by his hand and sat him down. "Deshawn, you are really gifted. Your abilities are from the Most High. You have the ability to not only alter reality from your dream state, but you have the power of the angels when you are in spirit form also. You really are the one! It's imperative that you always use your abilities for what's right," said Sarai.

"I will, but let's take a break. Are you hungry? I was thinking about meeting up with my bro and cuz. You know, just get out for a while. I would like for you to come with me. They are on St. Armand Circle at the—" Before Deshawn could get the word out, they were on St. Armand Circle. "That is soo cool," Deshawn said to Sarai. He looked at her to smile, but she wasn't smiling. She had an intense look on her face. Deshawn noticed that her wardrobe was different today. She had on all black with knee-high boots. It looked like she was wearing some type of superhero outfit.

Deshawn looked around for his cousin and his brother. He noticed two black Chevy Malibus with tinted windows pull up. There were four people in each car. Deshawn looked closer, and he saw Agent Nueman and Agent Holder in the separate cars. He looked over across the street and saw Zack and Andre. They cars windows rolled down. Deshawn said to Sarai, "There!" He pointed to Andre and Zack coming out of a store. Sarai teleported them there instantly.

"What the fuck?! I know for a fact you weren't standing here two seconds ago! Damn, you with the black Trinity?" said Zack.

"We gotta go!" yelled Deshawn. Gunshots starting ringing from the car. Sarai teleported everyone to Deshawn's living room within seconds.

"Is everyone OK?" Sarai asked.

Deshawn heard heavy breathing. He looked down and saw his cousin, Zack, had been shot and was bleeding heavily.

"Oh shit!" Andre yelled. Zack looked at Deshawn and Sarai as his life starting slipping away. He managed to get out a few words. "Do it, Deshawn, rewind it," he whispered.

To be continued ...